DISNEY

THE LION KING

Adapted by
JENNIFER LIBERTS

Illustrated by
THE DISNEY STORYBOOK ART TEAM

g A GOLDEN BOOK · NEW YORK

rhcbooks.com
ISBN 978-0-7364-3977-0
Printed in the United States of America
10 9 8 7 6 5 4 3 2 1

It was a proud day for King Mufasa and Queen Sarabi. Their newborn cub, Simba, had joined the great Circle of Life. One day Simba would take his father's place and become the Lion King.

Today the little cub was being presented to the entire animal kingdom. A wise old baboon named Rafiki marked the lion cub's forehead with red dust. Then he held Simba high in the air for all the animals to see.

Mufasa's brother, Scar, did not attend the celebration. He was angry that Simba was next in line to rule the kingdom. Scar had always wanted to be king.

Mufasa, disappointed in his younger brother, visited Scar's cave.

"Don't turn your back on me, Scar!" Mufasa growled.

Over time, Simba grew into a strong young cub. One morning, Mufasa took Simba to the top of Pride Rock.

"Everything the light touches is our kingdom," Mufasa explained. Simba was curious about the dark spot of land in the distance. Mufasa warned Simba never to go to the shadowy place beyond their borders. It was too dangerous.

Later that day, Simba saw Scar on a rocky ledge.

"Uncle Scar!" called Simba proudly. "Someday I'm gonna rule the whole kingdom! Well . . . everything except for the shadowy place."

"Right!" said Scar. "Only the bravest lions go there. An elephant graveyard is no place for a young prince."

Scar had set a dangerous trap for the young lion. He knew that Simba would want to prove he was brave. Sure enough, Simba ran off to ask his best friend, Nala, to go exploring with him.

Simba and Nala wandered into the Shadow Lands. Suddenly, they found themselves in the elephant graveyard, surrounded by three hyenas.

Zazu, the king's helper, heard the hyenas' evil laughter and flew down to protect Simba and Nala. Zazu stood between the hyenas and the cubs, but he was no match for the hungry hyenas. Simba and Nala were in trouble.

Just as the hyenas were about to attack, Mufasa leaped in front of
Simba, Nala, and Zazu. He had the hyenas cornered. Before the hyenas
could escape, Mufasa held them down with his powerful paws.

"Don't ever come near my son again!" he warned with a deep growl.

The hyenas ran away. Mufasa was angry that Simba had disobeyed him. Simba was sad that he had disappointed his father.

Mufasa led the cubs back to the Pride Lands. No one noticed Scar watching from the shadows. . . .

That night, Mufasa took Simba out to play in the grass. Mufasa knew Simba hadn't planned to put himself or Nala in danger, but he wanted to make sure he stayed safe.

"Being brave doesn't mean you go looking for trouble," he reminded his son.

Mufasa and Simba gazed at the stars.

"The great kings of the past look down on us from those stars," said Mufasa. "Whenever you feel alone, just remember that those kings will always be there to guide you. And so will I."

Meanwhile, Scar visited the hyenas at the elephant graveyard. He was angry that they'd let Simba go. He came up with a new wicked plan. This time, Simba and Mufasa would not get away.

The next day, Scar lured Simba to a deep gorge and told him to wait on a rock.

"Your father has a marvelous surprise for you," Scar lied before creeping away.

With Simba alone, Scar set his plan in motion. He told the hyenas to scare a herd of wildebeests. The frightened wildebeests stampeded—and headed right for Simba!

Scar ran to Mufasa and Zazu to tell them the cub was in danger. He led them into the gorge, where they saw Simba hanging from a tree branch!

"Hold on, Simba!" Mufasa cried.

Before Simba could fall beneath the pounding hooves of the wildebeests, Mufasa grabbed him. But as he carried his son away, a wildebeest knocked Mufasa to the ground.

Mufasa struggled to climb to safety, but his body was tired from running through the stampede. Scar saw him hanging from the edge of a cliff.

"Brother—help me!" pleaded Mufasa.
Scar dug his claws into Mufasa's paws and pulled him close.
"Long live the king," whispered Scar before he let Mufasa fall.

As the last of the wildebeests left the gorge, the dust settled. Simba could see his father lying still on the ground. He ran to his side.

"Dad? Dad, come on," Simba cried as he tried to wake Mufasa. "Get up."

Simba prodded the king with his paws over and over. He called his father's name and pulled at his ear, but Mufasa didn't move.

Simba curled up beside Mufasa and cried. He stayed there until he heard a voice calling him.

"Simba," Scar said coldly. "If it weren't for you, the king would still be alive. Run away, Simba. Never return!"

Simba ran and ran. Scar ordered the hyenas to get rid of Simba. They chased the cub all the way to the edge of a plateau. But when Simba leaped into a thorny patch of bushes below, the hyenas were too cowardly to follow.

"He's as good as dead anyway," they said as Simba escaped.

Simba walked for miles under the hot sun until he collapsed. Luckily, Timon the meerkat and Pumbaa the warthog found him and carried him to a water hole.

Simba told them that he could not go back to Pride Rock. Timon and Pumbaa took him to their home and even showed him how to eat bugs!

"This is a great life," said Timon. "No rules, no responsibilities, and no worries! **HAKUNA MATATA!**"

With the help of his new friends, Simba learned to live life with no worries. He grew into a strong young lion. But one night, as they gazed at the stars, Simba remembered his father's words.

"Someone once told me that the great kings of the past are up there, watching over us," he told Timon and Pumbaa sadly.

The next day, a lioness chased
Pumbaa through the jungle.
Simba pounced and the two lions
fought until the lioness pinned
Simba to the ground. Simba
looked into her eyes and
recognized . . .

"Nala!" he said. "It's me—Simba!"

"Simba?" Nala cried. "Everyone thought you were dead. But you're alive! And that means *you're* the king!"

Nala told Simba that cruel King Scar had ruined the Pride Lands. The animals were starving, and hyenas were everywhere.

Simba could claim the throne, but he was afraid to go back.

That night, the wise old baboon Rafiki came to see Simba.
He led Simba to a small pool where at first Simba saw only his
reflection. But then he saw his father's face in the water.
"You see," Rafiki said, "you are Mufasa's boy.
He lives in you."

At that very moment, Mufasa's image appeared in the clouds.
"You must take your place in the Circle of Life," Mufasa said.
"Remember who you are. You are my son, and the one true king."

Simba and his friends returned to the Pride Lands the following day. Simba was horrified to see that Scar had let the land go to ruin. No trees grew, and bones were scattered everywhere. His uncle had not respected the Circle of Life.

As Simba prepared to face Scar, his friends reminded him that they would always be by his side.

"We're with you till the end," Timon promised.

Meanwhile, Queen Sarabi had gone to speak with Scar. She told him that all the animals must leave Pride Rock— there was no food left. But Scar refused to listen.

Suddenly, Scar heard a deep roar. He turned and saw a huge lion.

"Mufasa?" he said fearfully. "But you're dead!"

"Mufasa?" Sarabi said, confused. Then she recognized the lion as her son. "Simba!"

Simba commanded Scar to step down or fight. "I've come back to take my place as king," Simba declared.

Scar was not willing to let his nephew take his throne. "It's your fault Mufasa's dead!" Scar said as he backed Simba toward the edge of Pride Rock.

Scar lunged at Simba and forced him off the cliff's end. As Simba struggled to hold on, Scar leaned over him. Lightning hit the ground and a fire began to burn around them.

"Now, this looks familiar," Scar said with an evil smile. "This is just the way your father looked before I killed him!"

Simba was immediately filled with rage. With all his
strength, he leaped at Scar, and they battled as the fire grew
around them. Scar fought hard to protect his place as king,
but he could not defeat Simba.

Simba chased Scar off the cliff. As Scar fell, Simba repeated
what Scar had told him all those years before: "Run away!
Run away and never return!"

Simba climbed to the top of Pride Rock. Rain fell from the sky, and he let it wash over him. He remembered his father and all he had learned from him. Simba held his head high and let out a powerful roar. At last, he was the Lion King.

Under Simba's rule, the Pride Lands once again became a place where herds came to graze and the trees grew strong and tall. And soon King Simba and Queen Nala had their own newborn cub for the kingdom to celebrate and welcome into the Circle of Life.

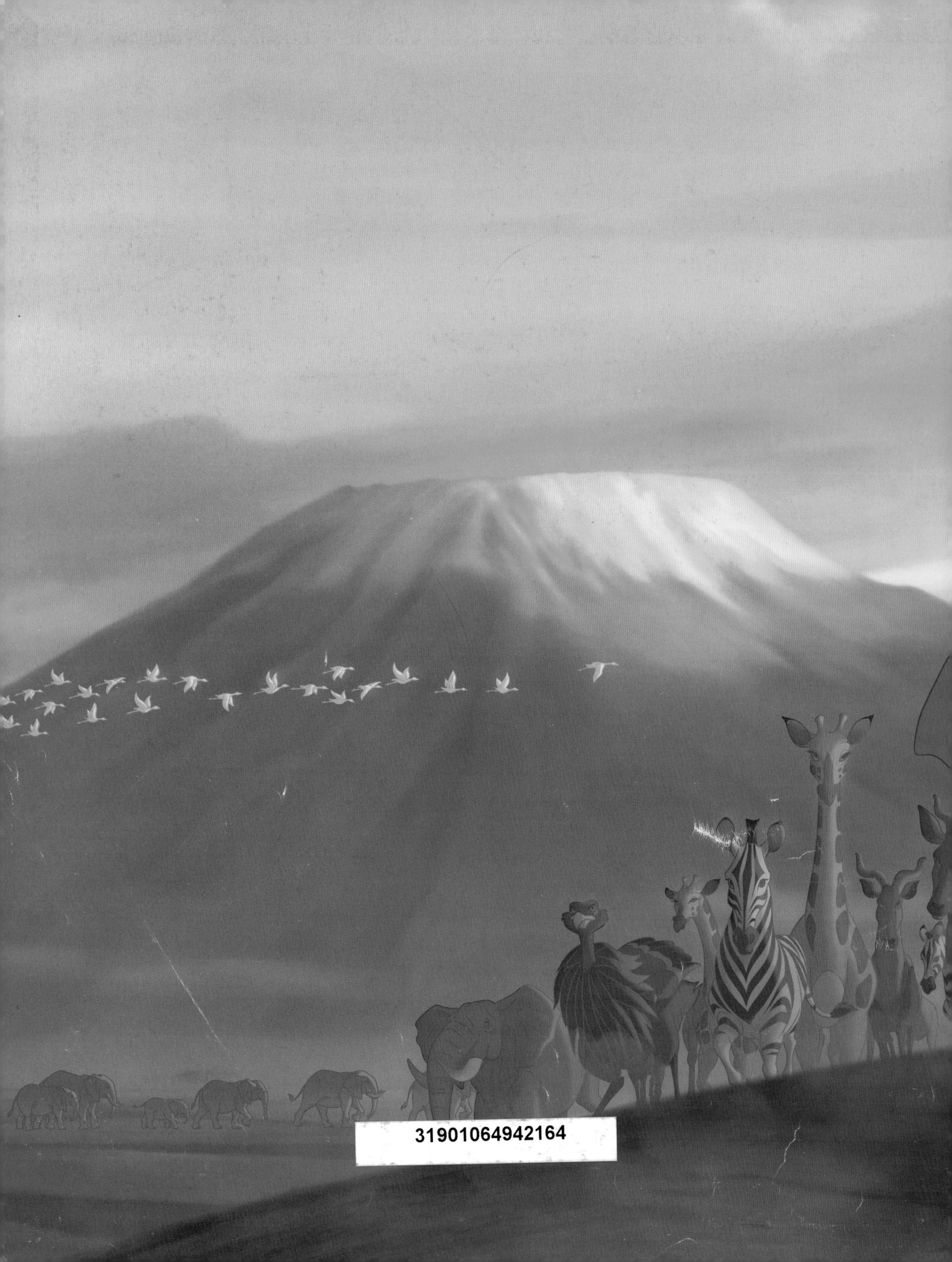